THE SWORD OF PRAXUS

The Sword of Praxus is a work of fiction. References to real people, events, establishments, organizations, or locales are intended only to provide the sense of authenticity and are use fictitiously. All other characters, all incidents, dialogue are drawn from the author's imagination and are not to be seen as real.

Copyright © 2022. All rights reserved.

Published by Dark Titan Publishing. A division of Dark Titan Entertainment.

Prodigious Worlds is an imprint of Dark Titan Entertainment.

Paperback ISBN: 979-8-9866393-7-6
eBook ISBN: 979-8-9866393-8-3

darktitanentertainment.com

WORKS BY TY'RON W. C. ROBINSON II

BOOKS/SHORT STORIES

DARK TITAN UNIVERSE SAGA

MAIN SERIES
Dark Titan Knights
The Resistance Protocol
Tales of the Scattered
Tales of the Numinous
Day of Octagon
Crossbreed
Heaven's Called
The Oranos Imperative
Underworld
Magicks & Mysticism

SPIN-OFFS
In A Glass of Dawn: The Casebook of Travis Vail
Maveth: Bloodsport
The Curse of The Mutant-Thing
Trail of Vengeance
War of The Thunder Gods

ONE-SHOTS
Maveth, The Death-Bringer Mystery of The Mutant-Thing Shade & Switchblade
Retribution of Cain
The Mythologists
Ambush Bot
Kang-Zhu
Cheeseburger Man
Tessa Balthazar
Elite 5

COLLECTIONS
Dark Titan Omnibus: Volume 1
Dark Titan Omnibus: Volume 2
Dark Titan One-Shot Collection
Dark Titan One-Shot Collection II

THE HAUNTED CITY SAGA
The Legendary Warslinger: The Haunted City I
Battle of Astolat: A Haunted City Prequel (KOBO Exclusive)
Redemption of the Lost: The Haunted City II
Helper's Hand: A Haunted City One-Shot
The Haunted City Collection

SYMBOLUM VENATORES
Symbolum Venatores: The Gabriel Kane Collection
Hod: A Symbolum Venatores Book
Symbolum Venatores: War of The Two Kingdoms Symbolum Venatores: Elrad's Chronicles
Symbolum Venatores Collection

EVERWAR UNIVERSE
EverWar Universe: Knights & Lords
Avior vs. Dekar

PRODIGIOUS WORLDS
Mark Porter of Argoron
Raiders of Vanok
Praxus of Lithonia
Prodigious Worlds: The First Worlds

FRIGHTENED! SERIES
Frightened!: The Beginning

INSTINCTS SERIES
Lost in Shadows: Remastered
Instincts Point Hope
The New Haven/Point Hope Incidens

THE HORDE TRILOGY
The Horde
The Dreaded Ones

DARK TITAN'S THE DEAD DAYS
Accounts of The Dead Days

OTHER BOOKS
The Book of The Elect
The Extended Age Omnibus
The Eleventh Hour: A Chevah Mythos Story
The Supreme Pursuer: Darkness of the Hunt
Massacre in the Dusk
Venture into Horror: Tales of the Supernatural
The Universe of Realms Omnibus: Book 1
The Universe of Realms Omnibus: Book 2

THE DARK TITAN AUDIO EXPERIENCE PODCAST
Season 1: Introductions
Season 2: In a Glass of Dawn
Season 2.5: Accounts of The Dead Days
Season 3: Battle For Astolat
Season 4: Hallow Sword: Cursed

THE SWORD OF PRAXUS

TY'RON W. C. ROBINSON II

CONTENTS

CHAPTER ONE: THE JOURNEY BEGINS AGAIN
1

CHAPTER TWO: THE VALLEY OF THE LOST
5

CHAPTER THREE: THE WALK AMONGST THE MOUNTAINS
10

CHAPTER FOUR FIGHT FOR THE SWORD
14

CHAPTER FIVE: DUEL WITH THE BLADE
19

- AN EXCERPT FROM THE GODS AND MEN OF ARGORON ++++++++++++++++++++++++23
- NEW ORDER OF THE WORLD: AN EVERWAR UNIVERSE STORY _____25

CHAPTER ONE: THE JOURNEY BEGINS AGAIN

Through the land of Lithonia, word had spread of Praxus' victory against King Bantos and his Bandorian forces alongside King Brithon and the Brithonians. The people cheered Praxus as their champion. From then on, the rule of Bantos continued to grow deeper. The oppression spread throughout the regions. With Praxus as their savior, the people relied on him to end Bantos' rule. However, that time would only come if Praxus and Bantos were standing in the same room. A rare occasion as Bantos decreased his outdoor presence amongst his subjects.

On a ride out into the market, Praxus greeted the people as they cheered him on. While riding through the market, a conversation caught his ear. Praxus jumped from his horse and walked toward the two men speaking in the shade of the tent. Praxus approached them, startling him by his great stature.
"You're him."
"I'm whom?" Praxus asked.
"The Savior. The one who will free us all from Bantos' rule."
"Ah. Bantos' empire will fall soon. However, I've come because I overheard your conversation. You spoke of a sword."
"Not just any kind of sword. The Skeldergate Sword."

Praxus nodded at the sound. Yet, he's never heard of such a blade. The two men continued to tell Praxus of its history and its last known location. From there, Praxus sought out to retrieve this legendary sword as a means of defeating Bantos completely.

Unknown to Praxus, Bantos had learned of the Skeldergate Sword due to his soldiers patrolling the land. The same men told the soldiers of the weapon and they returned to Bantos, giving him the details. Intrigued by the sound of this sword, Bantos sent out word for a mercenary to track down the weapon. Several days later, a mercenary appeared at the doors of Bantos' kingdom. Armored in thick leather. Tall stature. His stare intimidated even the soldiers of the palace. The soldiers led this brute of a man into the throne room and when Bantos saw him, his eyes widen. He knew just by the sheer presence of the mercenary. He would be the one to retrieve the sword.

"State your name." Bantos said.

"Jax. Jax The Annihilator."

"The Annihilator? Well, such a name fits a being of your stature. Tell me, why have you chosen to come to this quest? What do you wish to gain from it?"

"Glory. Purpose. Before coming here, I was just a mercenary who accepted tasks with low pay. I would occasionally enter the gladiatorial events to show off my strength and fighting style. Yet, much was not given to me. But to hear of a legendary sword being kept in the far mountains. It has me intrigued deeply. Finally, a chance to prove myself to the highest order of life."

"You seek much from this quest." Bantos noted. "However, your demeanor proves you're a capable warrior. Before you go on this quest, I must warn you. There is another man out there who is also seeking the sword. He is an enemy of mine. It would do you even better if you manage to slay this man and claim the sword. If that is done, glory and purpose shall be yours with much more to follow."

"May I ask the name of this enemy?"

"The people call him Praxus of Lithonia."

Jax nodded.

"It will be done."

Bantos nodded with a wave of the hand as Jax left the throne room to begin the quest for the sword.

The following morning as Praxus was preparing his horse for the journey, he was visited by King Brithon and a few of his warriors. They greeted Praxus like brothers. Brithon noticed the horse carrying objects such for water and food. He looked toward Praxus as he placed his sword and sheath on the horse's side.

"Where are you heading?"

"There is a sword hidden deep in the mountains. I intend on finding it."

"Ah. You speak of the famed Skeldergate Sword."

"You know of it?"

"I do. I even attempted to capture the blade myself. Although, I underestimated the amount of sinister forces that drive men out of the path. I was too young at the time."

"What sinister forces do you speak of?"

"Ghouls. Monsters. Some even said they saw demons. I only came into contact with the ghouls. Took some of them out with my sword. But there were too many of them for me to kill. So, I fled. Never returned."

Praxus gave Brithon a nod. The Brithrowian king knew Praxus believed he could accomplish the goal. Praxus leaped atop his horse, set forth to ride out into the unknown.

"When you get back," Brithon said. "make sure to aid us with that sword."

"Will do." Praxus nodded.

Praxus rode out from his homestead, giving a nod and a war

cry yell toward Brithon and his warriors as a symbol of brotherhood. Brithon watched as Praxus rode out toward the unknown where the mountains are darker and the sky is lower.

CHAPTER TWO: THE VALLEY OF THE LOST

Praxus left the land of the dwelling as he entered the wasteland of the wilderness. Trees were no more to be seen as tall as they were. The grass beneath his feet withered away after each gallop from the horse. The sky darkened after each breath. Praxus knew he was now in unknown territory. The wind touched his face with a cold kiss. Yet, Praxus was not afraid as he could hear the sounds of echoes coming from afar. Echoes not of the humankind. Screechy. Bellowing. Monstrous. Praxus stepped from his horse and raised his sword as the low pitch of growls approached. Praxus waited as through the thick fog emerged three wolves. However, these wolves were beyond the size of the average wolf which dwell in the nearby lands of the cities.

Praxus raised his sword. His feet set as the wolves circled the Lithonian. The horse was no fazed nor bothered by the wolves. The wolves neither gave attention toward the horse nor did they pose as a threat. Their sights were only locked on Praxus. Which the Lithonian figured to be strange in his case. As if the wolves were sent for him and him alone.

"Are you going to attack or remain standing still?" Praxus said.

The wolves only glared as their eyes glinted with the shrouded sunlight. The first wolf went for the attack, only to be slashed by Praxus' blade. The wolf paused itself as it slowly stepped and fell. The second wolf went next. Its jaws nearly snatching the sword from Praxus' grasp. Praxus turned as quick as possible, kicking the large beast in its side before taking the sword and impaling it into the ribs of the wolf. Praxus pulled the sword from the wolf's body as its blood covered the blade completely. The insides of the wolf slowly leaked through onto the dirt. Only one wolf remained and the Lithonian was prepared. The wolf howled and ran back into the fog. With a sigh of relief, Praxus sheath the sword and returned to his horse, continuing on his journey toward the mountains.

While Praxus continued through the valley to reach the mountains, Jax followed and slaughtered the remaining wolf in his path.

Praxus continued down the path and as he did, he was attacked by more creatures. This time, a group of hybrid-beasts. Creatures who appeared human from the bottom and animalistic from the top. One appeared tot be a leopard-man whom Praxus quickly dealt with by the swipe of his sword. The other was a goat-man. Praxus snatched the horns of the creatures and slammed it into the ground before burying the sword into its neck. The third was hog-man and the fourth was a bear-man. Praxus grinned as they rushed toward him. Moving past them with such speed, Praxus impaled the hog-man in the back and slashed the throat of the bear-man. The hybrid beasts were no more and Praxus continued on his journey. Jax had come to the scene and saw the bodies in the dirt. He scoffed with a grin on his face as he gazed forward.

The night had fallen and Praxus settled, finding a small cavern to dwell in for the night. The horse rested near the entrance as Praxus sat in front of the fire, pondering the journey.

"With that sword, I can end Bantos' rule." Praxus said in his mind. *"I can liberate my people. Liberate Brithon's people. Save this land."*

Praxus laid down and slept. Hours had passed and Praxus found himself awoken to the sound of a rushing wind. He jolted from the ground with his palm on the hilt of his sword. His head spinning, searching every spot of the cavern. He gazed toward the entrance, only to see his horse still resting as it there was no wind. Praxus questioned the source of the wind and as he sighed, he turned around and found himself staring in the face of a ghoul. Misty as a cloud, yet its eyes dark as obsidian stone. Praxus was not afraid as he stared back into the eyes of the ghoul.

"Do not fear, Lithonian." The Ghoul spoke.

"How do you know me?"

"I am aware of your purpose here. You seek the Skeldergate Sword."

"I do. And from your tone, you know the precise location of this sword in the Megarian Mountains."

"I do. I have seen the blade myself."

"This still doesn't question why you're come t bother me during my rest."

"I've come to warn you, Lithonian. The sword is not some mere weapon like the one you're holding. No. the Skeldergate Sword is a weapon of true power. Without a pure heart, the sword will corrupt its wielder and send them down the path of destruction."

"You know this how?"

"I was once its wielder. Many ages ago during the War of the Chosen. The blade served me well, yet in the end I became a victim to it and fell in the process. The blade was sent into the mountains, surrounded by fire conjured by a sorcerer to make sure no one gets their hands on it. No one."

Praxus nodded toward the Ghoul. Taking in his words carefully.

"I understand your concern. However, I am not like the others who have come and gone before me. I am destined to take down Bantos and his empire. The Skeldergate blade will serve me in accomplishing my purpose."

"I warn you. Do not think yourself as highly as you ought not. I was once in your place. I know the outcome of pride when it overtakes you."

"It is not pride that I speak from. It is from experience. It is from prophecy."

The Ghoul hovered back as if it lost a step.

"Prophecy? What prophecy has spoken of a Lithonian bringing down the Bandorian Empire?"

"One" Praxus answered. "And I am what will bring down Bantos' reign."

"You sound sure of your prophecy."

"I am positive it will come to pass. If Bantos is not taken down, his empire will continue to slaughter and misuse the innocent. He will travel to the Farlands and seek to conquer their lands and their people. I cannot allow him to attempt such a tragedy."

The Ghoul showed respect toward Praxus and his purpose of seeking the sword. The Ghoul looked out toward the cavern entrance as it saw the glint of the sun peeking through the clouds. Morning had come.

"I will be watching you on your journey, Praxus of Lithonia."

"Do what you must, spirit." Praxus answered. "You shall see the actions come to pass."

With the sunlight starting to peek into the cavern, the Ghoul vanished through the burning smoke. Praxus arose and gathered himself as his horse waited for him at the entrance. Praxus stepped outside into the sunlight an sighed. He continued down the path as the peak of the mountains could be seen in the distance.

Some mere hours later, Jax had arrived at the sight of the cavern and proceeded to search the interior. All he found was the remains of the fire Praxus had made and he grinned. Stepping back out of the cavern and looking toward the mountains ahead.
"I'm on to you, Lithonian."

CHAPTER THREE: THE WALK AMONGST THE MOUNTAINS

Praxus rode for hours, several breaks in between his travels as the skies became darker as he inched closer toward the Megarian Mountains. The fog grew from beneath, shrouding the sight of the desert dirt. The stench in the air became as unbearable to the dead. Praxus saw the mountain ahead and rode to reach it. The horse galloped with such speed, the smell of the air evaporated from Praxus' nose. He could breathe calmly for once during his recent moves. The horse stopped as Praxus glared up, seeing the mountain fully. A colossal structure. Burnt like through a furnace. Near the peak of the mountain came smoke.

"The sword is there."

Praxus stepped from his horse and grabbed his sword. Walking up toward the mountain. As he walked, he noticed a pattern carved through the rocks. A set of stairs. Praxus nodded as he continued his walk. Taking the stairs up the mountain, the air around him had a sense of knowing. Praxus' right hand on the handle of his blade. A sharp gust of wind moved past him, Praxus turned with intensity, his hand gripping the blade tighter. Praxus looked around the sitars, nothing in his sight. From there, he continued upward as more gusts came after ten steps. The closer he reached the peak, the more intense the winds became.

"Who's here with me?" Praxus spoke. "I know I am not alone."

The winds returned and while they moved past Praxus, in front of him an image began to form. In his sight, it appeared the wind had begun to manifest into a living being. Praxus raised his sword as he stared toward the forming image.

"Are you the ghoul from the cave? Have you followed me here to the mountains to test me? To watch my work? To see if I would complete my quest in full?"

"The cave?" A voice spoke from the winds. "We have not encountered one such as you."

"Reveal yourself." Praxus demanded. "Show yourself to me in full."

The strength of the winds increased, nearly knocking Praxus backwards down the steps. Holding his balance as the winds continued, through them Praxus could make out the formations of several beings. Their expressions appeared human, however their eyes shined like fine silver. Sparkling in like fashion of the night stars. Their flowing ghostly hair was white as snow. Each of the spirits were fashioned in long robe apparel. A mixture of the snowy peaks from above and the dust below.

"You stand before the Spirits of the Air! We have made ourselves known to you." The front Spirit said. "Who are you?"

"I am Praxus of Lithonia. I have come to this mountain to retrieve the Skeldergate Sword."

The Spirit glanced down toward Praxus' right hand. Seeing him wielding his sword.

"You already possess a blade. Why seek out another?"

"This is an ordinary blade I carry. What I've heard concerning the Skeldergate Sword intrigues me. I can wield it and save my people from King Bantos' rule and aid others across the world who need such help."

"You desire to help those in need. We speak with one who desires to do good rather than evil."

"You do." Praxus confirmed.

"How can we trust this stranger?" One of the other Spirits spoke. "He is human like the others."

"Indeed he is. Yet, there's something about this one that is different than those from past times. Something within his spirit calls for justice. Mercy. Deliverance. Such attributes are what is needed in these times."

The spirits gathered themselves together and spoke silently. Praxus stood still, unable to hear the words exhale from the mouths of the spirits. The spirits continued to speak and each nodded in single fashion toward the other. They moved back from one another and turned to face Praxus.

"What have you said of me?"

"We have come to the agreement to let you pass."

"And why is that?"

"Your spirit. There is good within you. Use it well and if you're capable of retrieving the sword from its fiery place, best use it for the good of all living."

Praxus nodded in thankfulness.

"I shall do as such."

The spirits disappeared from the Lithonian's sights as if they were never in his presence. With his sword sheathed, Praxus continued upward as he came closer toward the pillaring smoke.

In the distance behind him, Jax walked up the stairs and came into contact with the spirits. They questioned him in similar methods. But, Jax was not one of a good spirit in their sights.

"Do you heed our words, mercenary?" The Spirit spoke. "Your arrogance oozes from your being. The pride which is in you will only cause you to fall."

"My pride, spirit, will grant me my rewards. I will be a king amongst men in all the lands."

"Men who speak in such a fashion shall not achieve what they desire. Only the dust of the ground shall you be rewarded for your recklessness."

Jax grinned and slammed his sword into the ground, starling the spirits as he waved it around, moving the spirits around the spot, causing them to flee.

"Do I seem afraid of you all?! Now, who are the ones that flee the conflict?! Not I!"

One of the spirits went for an attack on Jax, only for his blade to whither them like mist in the morning. With the other spirits gone, Jax roared a scream of victory as he plunged his sword into the rocky ground.

"Reckless spirits." Jax spat out. "I am not like those who've come before you. I am Jax the Annihilator!"

With a keen gaze upward, Jax saw the flowing dark smoke. He grinned as a slight chuckle exited from his mouth. He sheathed his blade and followed the stairs upward.

CHAPTER FOUR FIGHT FOR THE SWORD

Praxus had continued further up the mountain as the smoke was growing darker after every step. The air began to be consumed by the flowing smoke. With one final staircase, Praxus went up and once he placed his foot on the top step, he saw in front of him the Skeldergate Sword. Completely surrounded by the flames which created the pillar of smoke. The sword glistened with a gold texture. The hilt shined like fine silver pulled from the furnace. Praxus approached the flames of the sword and stretch forth his hand. The heat intensified as he pulled back. Slightly grunting from the burn.

"It seems you've reached a dead end." a voice said behind Praxus.

The Lithonian turned to see Jax. Standing boldly with his sword in hand. Praxus pulled out his own sword in defense as the flames sparked behind him. Jax grinned as his eyes were set on Praxus.

"Bantos sent you here?" Praxus asked. "To kill me I presume."

"Not just that. He wants that blade as well. Plus, he offered me a fine payment that I could not refuse."

"To use it to enslave others under his rule."

"I don't care what Bantos seeks to do after he has the sword. I only care about my payment."

Jax raised his sword and impaled it into the ground with a roaring yell, commanding Praxus to stand aside. Praxus did not move.

"You're sure you want to die here? Atop this forsaken mountain by the gods?!"

"I will not be the one to die today." Praxus declared.

Jax with a grunt from his mouth lunged toward Praxus with his blade forward. Praxus stepped aside as his sword clashed with Jax's own. Jax moved with force, slamming his sword against the steel of Praxus. Praxus had no choice but to use his mobility of speed to swoop past the attacks from Jax. The swords continued to clash with one another. Jax's strength had surpassed Praxus by a few meters, however the Lithonian had enough energy to contain his deflections and retaliate with his own attacks, slashing Jax in the left thigh.

"You think a cut can defeat me?!"

"Never had a thought."

Jax dropped his sword and rushed toward Praxus with his bare hands. Delivering a series of blows with his fists into the abdomen and chest of the Lithonian. Praxus stumbled from the attacks and shook himself back to focus. Seeing the next punch coming, Praxus moved and grabbed the right arm of Jax and held it tightly, falling to the ground into a armbar. Jax yelled as he was locked in.

"Is this your best?!"

"You won't be using this arm anytime soon."

With a bend, Praxus broke Jax's arm from the elbow down. The Annihilator screamed in pain as Praxus let him go and stepped back from the brute warrior. And yet, Jax arose from the ground, shook himself back to focus. He grinned as if the pain had subsided.

"I cannot be stopped! I am Jax the Annihilator!"

Praxus sighed, gripping his sword.

"Let's end this before you embarrass yourself further."

Jax ran toward the Lithonian with his fists ready to strike, Praxus ducked the double attack and swiped his sword into the back of Jax. The brute warrior paused in his stels as he felt to one knee. Praxus took another slash toward Jax's back and he fell to both knees. Praxus went and stood in front of him as Jax raised his head to see him.

"Two swipes in the back, huh. Never expected you to attack a warrior from behind."

"I ducked and went for the strike. I'm not behind you am I."

Jax sighed as he spit blood.

"Finish it. Do it before my strength returns and I shatter your skull with my hands."

Praxus held up his blade and impaled Jax in the heart. The brute fell to his death and Praxus turned his focus back to the sword. Sheathing his own blade, Praxus approached the flames, seeking to find a way to rid of the fire. Praxus picked up dirt from the ground and threw it into the flames, seeing the dirt burn before it even reached the interior of the fires. Such sight caught Praxus off guard.

"This fire is not made of natural origins."

Praxus took his sword and touch the flames with it, seeing how the steel slowly began to burn from the flames.

"The flames. This is only caused by-"

"Magic." a voice spoke from behind.

Praxus turned quickly, believing Jax to have risen from the dead. Only to find himself staring at the same man he met in the cave sometime past. Praxus held his sword steady toward the hooded figure.

"You're back." Praxus said. "Dakin Maul was it?"

"You haven't forgotten me." Dakin grinned as he was crouched atop the rocks of the mountain. "Good. Good."

"Why are you here? Was it you who communed with the ghoul to speak to me in the cave? To bring the Spirits of the Air to test my spirituality?"

"I did none of what you've spoken. I am simply here to make sure you complete the task set before you."

"You are aware of my quest to retrieve this warsword?"

"I know many things, Lithonian. Such you cannot possibly imagine with your finite mind."

Praxus sheathed his blade as he pointed toward the Skeldergate Sword. Dakin turned his sights toward it and nodded with a relaxed gesture of the shoulders.

"These flames are made of magic. I cannot bring them down."

"I know."

"Tell me how I can rid the flames from the sword and retrieve it?"

"And why should I tell you the secret to the sword?"

"Because if you don't, I'll kill you where you stand."

Dakin let out a sinister laugh before raising his right hand, causing the sword in Praxus' had o increase in weight. Praxus being unable to hold the sword, dropped it near his feet as Dakin's light ceased immediately.

"I am not the one to pose forward threats, Lithonian."

Praxus stared toward Dakin, wanting to strike and yet seeing a small fraction of the warlock's power, he did not know how to combat him in a straight fight. Dakin waived his hand.

"There is no need for us to battle. Not this day."

"Then, help me with the flames. Rid them from the ground that I may claim the blade."

"If I help you, will you sheath the blade once you have it in your possession? Will you not make an attack on me?"

"I will not. As you said, not this day."

Dakin grinned and raised his hands, moving them down

slowly. Praxus turned to the flames and saw they were descending into the ground just as Dakin moved his hands. Within seconds, the flames were gone and only small fragments of ash and embers remained. Dakin pointed toward the sword.

"There. Claim your prize."

Praxus focused his strength and grabbed the Skeldergate Sword, pulling it from his slumbering lock with all he had within him and raised it to the sky as a crack of thunder echoed the retrieving. Dakin watched as Praxus suddenly grew in power thanks to the sword. *There's more to the weapon than what is told.*

"It seems your quest is complete, Lithonian." Dakin said. "We shall meet again."

"And I will be ready."

Dakin nodded with a smile as he vanished through a rush of blue flames. Praxus sighed and glanced down, noticing Jax's body was also gone. He didn't mind it as he returned to his horse and rode off from the mountains, returning to civilization.

CHAPTER FIVE: DUEL WITH THE BLADE

Praxus made his return to civilization, making his first stop in Brithrow. Upon his arrival, he caught the glimpse of the Brithrowian army readying themselves for a battle. He knew it was against Bantos' forces. He rode into the city and reached the castle. Exiting from the castle doors in armor was King Brithon. Sheathing his sword as he saw Praxus enter the gates.

"The Lithonian makes his return!"

"I have. With something of value."

Praxus leaped from his horse and reached onto the side, pulling out the Skeldergate Sword. The army stumbled at its appearance. Sensing something otherworldly from the blade. Brithon however was intrigued. His eyes locked on the steel. Extending his hand, he touched the blade and felt its smoothness. A touch unlike the swords he and his soldiers wield.

"I never believe the sword actually existed." Brithon chuckled. "Tell me, how did you manage to retrieve it?"

"A sorcerer was present at the mountains."

"A sorcerer? There hasn't been one of them in the region for centuries."

"He's dwelling in the mountains. The same one was also present inside the caves near the battlegrounds from the last attack against Bantos."

"So, we have a warlock lurking around our lands. This is not good. I will do what I can to keep my eyes on anything unusual."

"I told him we shall meet again." Praxus sighed. "He continued to insist our lives would cross paths again and end in a battle between magic and might."

"Let us hope you wield that new blade when that battle does come."

"He knows I will."

Praxus sheathed the blade, calming the soldiers around him.

"Also, Bantos knew of the blade and its location."

"Bantos? How would he know?"

"He sent one of his mercenaries to find it as well. No need to concern yourself, I dealt with him in battle."

"Good of you. Now, as you can see, myself and the army are preparing to take down a garrison of Bantos' forces. They've managed to invade my land even more. We could use a helping hand. If you mind a little bloodshed."

With only a nod, Praxus agreed.

The battlefield was cloudy with mist as the garrison of Bantos' soldiers waited patiently for the arrival of Brithon and his men. The soldiers of Bantos sung song f their intended victory. Others danced on the field. They continued until hearing the galloping of horses in the distance. Preparing themselves as they saw in the distance Brithon and his army. A few of the soldiers present felt a sense of resurgence as the scenery seemed familiar to the last battle between themselves and Brithrow.

"Arm yourselves!" The General screamed.

Brithon's army arrived on the field and without hesitation the battle began. The ground became quickly drenched in the blood of men. Swords clashed and fell. Horses galloped and ran. Brithon looked out toward the pathways and grinned. He turned to see the

General of Bantos' army and pointed outward.

"Your defeat has arrived!"

Entering the battlefield was Praxus on his own horse. He stepped atop the galloping animal and lunged into the fight, slashing away at Bantos' soldiers with the Skeldergate Sword. The blade glistened in the sunlight and stunned the armies of both sides. Praxus looked at the blade and saw the General.

"What such weapon do you wield, Barbarian?!"

"One that will ensure Bantos' demise."

The General commanded all his soldiers to attack Praxus and him only. Brithon's soldiers went to interfere, and yet were told to stand down by Brithon. He knew something was about to take place. Praxus was surrounded by the soldiers. Their hands gripped to their swords as Praxus' own. Praxus grinned and permitted them the first attack. The soldiers did not hesitate as they all lunged toward the Lithonian and with one quick swipe around, Praxus decapitated the first several soldiers with the blade. The sight brought the General into a still of fear. Now the other soldiers had second thoughts about attacking Praxus.

"Brithon!" Praxus yelled. "Get your men to cover!"

"Cover?! Of what?!"

"You will see."

The General stepped into the fight and raised his sword. His presence in the field removed the fear from his soldiers as they surrounded Praxus.

"We will take him out and bring his head to Bantos!"

The General and his soldiers all went for the strike. Praxus nodded as he lifted up the Skeldergate Sword and plunged it into the ground. The impact created an earthquake which rocked the field, knocking the soldiers to the ground. Praxus yelled as he pulled the sword from the ground and once he did, the field was emerged in flames. Supernatural flames that consumed the General and his soldiers. The screams of the burning men brought joy toward Brithon and his soldiers. Praxus stood firm as he watched the soldiers fall to their deaths. Being burned alive.

"It is done." Praxus said, sheathing the blade.

With it sheathed, the fires vanished as if they were never present. Even the cracks in the ground from the earthquake had disappeared. Brithon saw this with his own eyes and was astonished. He walked over to Praxus, pointing at the sword.

"That is a powerful weapon you now possess."

"Yes. I still have a lot to learn of its use."

"One thing's for sure. That blade will bring an end to Bantos' rule and his empire of tyranny. I hope you're prepared to bring justice to this land."

"I am."

With word spreading across the land of Praxus' retrieval of the Skeldergate Sword, King Bantos paced back and forth in his war room as his servants arrived. Bantos sighed, overlooking a map of the land. Seeing his kingdom, Brithon's kingdom, and the others.

"Any word?" Bantos asked.

"We've received word from Alter-Nimrod. He accepts your proposal for war. He is ready to strike when you see fit."

Bantos grinned.

"Good. Send out word to the others. It will take nearly all kingdoms of this continent to bring down Brithrow and Praxus. Since he's retrieved the magic blade."

"Yes, my lord."

The servant exited the war room and Bantos placed a figurine of himself standing in the vast deserts of the land.

"The wars are truly about to begin."

AN EXCERPT FROM THE GODS AND MEN OF ARGORON

Mark Porter of Earth stared at the living light which was present before him.

"You are what?" Porter asked again.

"You heard what I said. I am a God of Argoron."

"Sorry. But I'm not familiar with the gods of this planet. I just came here not long ago."

"I know. I know."

"You know?"

"I saw the portal which brought you to this planet. I am aware of your homeworld. Your kind call it Earth, yes?"

"We do. How do you know of Earth?"

"Again. I am a God of Argoron. We know many things."

Porter moved around the area, his eyes locked on the light entity.

"Tell me this. What kind of god are you?"

"What do you mean?"

"What are you the god of?"

"If I would tell you, you would not be pleased nor calm."

"You're an evil one?"

"Evil? No, Earthman. I am a savior. A savior to this planet and its inhabitants. Yet, they refuse to hear my words. My guidelines for peace."

"Then appear before them reasonably and maybe they'll give you an ear to hear."

The light flickered as the sound of a door creaked open. Porter turned and saw Princess Lola Arribel approaching him, still covered in her white sleeping robe from the shoulders down to her feet. He quickly returned his sight toward the light entity, only to find the light dimmed and gone.

"Porter. What are you doing out here?"

"I came to get some air and there was, there was some king of being made of light."

"A being made of light?"

"Yes. It told me it was a god of this planet."

Lola paused. With a gentle nod, she returned inside and Porter followed.

AVAILABLE NOVEMBER 25, 2022

NEW ORDER OF THE WORLD: AN EVERWAR UNIVERSE STORY

A corridor confined with metallic walls. Silent. Streams of white smoke emit from the steel-plated floors and ceiling. Down the hallway, the echoing sounds of tapping. The tapping morphed into beating and through the smoke a young man who is called Timothy. Dressed in all black with a long sleeve shirt and jeans. Wearing boots. Timothy is sweating and is running in the sight of fear. His life at the present moment is depending on his speed. Behind him we see four silhouettes after him. The silhouette later manifest into a guard. They're known as the Realm Guards. Soldiers of the City and loyal to their leader. Donned in black armored uniforms, carrying high-powered artillery firearms diverse from single ranges to plasma-ranges, weapons similar to the rainshockers of the Viper Realm. Their faces shrouded by their black masks and goggles. Resembling reapers. No emotion can be seen from them. They chase down Timothy through the corridor. Timothy keeps running and stops at a nearby room. He enters the room as quickly as he could run. Timothy took a small moment to catch his breath. Though, he can still hear the footsteps of the guards coming near the room. Timothy looked around and found himself in the presence of a robot. The robot is modeled after human structure, equipped with the A.I. from the technologies in the land. The name of the robot is A14-12.

"You appear to be in a rush."

"The Realm Guards are after me." Timothy said, catching his breath. "I need to get rid of them."

"Now why would I assist you?"

"To keep them from killing me."

The robot examined Timothy and his garments.

"You're one of them."

Timothy nodded quickly. A14-12 recognized his intentions.

"Give me a moment."

Timothy waits for A14-12 to assist him, hearing the footsteps of the guards growing. Inching near him. Sweat drops from Timothy's forehead.

"They're coming closer!"

"Have some patience with me. After all, your kind know of patience."

A14-12 approaches Timothy with a device. The robot hands it to him. Timothy looks at it, unknown to what it is. He looks over at A14-12, questioning.

"What is this?" Timothy waved.

"If you want to evade the guards, hold it above your head."

Timothy scanned the device. Intrigued by its design.

"Is this some kind of teleporter?"

"No. They don't place them within this room. What you're holding will be good enough for your sudden cause."

The guards are near as their voices can be heard in the distance. Timothy holds the device above his head. A silver-colored mist fell from the device around him. Timothy notices himself becoming transparent. His flesh vanishing before his eyes. He knows he's becoming invisible. The guards burst into the room. Guns in hand. They circle the room, seeing only A14-12 standing. Calm demeanor for a robot. One guard approaches him. Eyes locked on tight.

"Mechroid, have you seen an enashian run past here?"

"I have not. You're the first I've seen this day."

"If you encounter the enashian, alert the Highguard."

"I will do that."

The guards leave the room and move further down the corridor. A14-12 looked around, scanning the room. Through the scanning process, the robot could see the invisible Timothy standing against the wall.

"Ah. There you are."

The robot grabbed a small firearm from the table and fired an electric bolt toward Timothy. The bolt hits Timothy in his left knee. He jolts and becomes visible again with the electric currents revealing himself.

"Why did you do that?!"

"You didn't make yourself visible, so I had to do it."

Timothy shook his head with a slight nod.

"Thanks."

Its not a problem. But, since you're here and finding your way out of this land. I assume you're on your way to finding the other renegades.

"The others?" Timothy jolted, waving his hands in disagreement. "No. No. I'm just trying to get out of this place with what I know."

"But, you're an enashian."

Timothy paused . The mechroid is aware Timothy isn't understanding the meaning of his words.

It's better of you to find them. You can lead them here to save the enashians and mechroids from the tyranny we live under.

"Why are you so interested in all of this?"

"I have my own reasons."

Timothy takes it in. Seeing what appears to be some form of character within the robot. A care perhaps? Unsure as to where the renegades may be.

"I'm on my way out of here anyway." Timothy let out a faint

sigh. "I'll try to find the renegades."

"Maybe they'll find you."

"I'll take your word for it."

Timothy walks toward the door.

"We'll see once I get back. If I make it back."

"You'll be well." A14 said with certainty.

Timothy had left the room, running through the corridor and finding the exit. He exited the corridor and continued running.

Timothy runs outside of the base, he looks around, seeing himself surrounded by techno-buildings and flying drones made of beaten down metals. The buildings were as tall as skyscrapers and the air was lukewarm. The sounds of an electrical howling can be heard roaming in the skies above him. The city itself was one with great heaviness and astounding beauty. The structure looked to have been built many years ago. The aging itself had no greater effect than to instill fear. Its scent was of a burning fire mixed with electricity and a strange catch of cinnamon. He could hear the faint, yet squealing sounds of humans screaming coming from within the city. Their screams were of torment. It irked him, making his escape and finding himself entering the wilderness.

Timothy walks through the wilderness, known to those around the area as the Desolate. Nothing can be seen but a vast desert. Sand and rocks sit in places. Trees little to none. Few cactuses stood apart form each other. Scattered. Timothy walks through the Desolate as the wind slowly picks up and dust flies through the air. Timothy covers his face with his arm to avoid having sand fly into his eyes, nose, and mouth. He keeps walking as the wind increases in strength. The heat has increased in temperature and it begins to tire Timothy out. Yet, he continues moving through. After walking several more feet from his previous location, Timothy appears to spot a small structure up ahead.

"Is that a base?" Timothy glared.

As he goes to take another step, Timothy is stopped and

lassoed from behind. Timothy looks down at the lasso around his torso. Hearing what is someone running toward him from behind, he turns his head, only to see a fist flying towards him. The fist punches Timothy, knocking him unconscious. Timothy awoke with a jolt. Beginning to regain his senses. Now knowing he's sitting down and his arms tied behind the chair. He's aware he's sitting in the middle of a room. The room is dark and the only light source he can see is coming from the sun above him through a circular hole in the ceiling. The room, of what Timothy could see was dirty with the Desolate sand. It smelled of vehicular oil and sweat. Its odor bothered Timothy, but he kept himself focused. Timothy tried looking around the room, seeing no one. He questions the scenario. He's tied up, so there must be someone within the room with him.

"OK." Timothy looked around. "This is strange. Anyone in here?"

No sound of a reply returns to him. Timothy quieted himself. Taking in a breath.

"Hello! Is there anyone in here besides me?! I'm pretty sure there is!

Footsteps are heard in front of Timothy. Though, he cannot see who's walking as they are shrouded in the thick darkness surrounding him. The footsteps come closer and more footsteps are heard. They are surrounding Timothy and he knows it. Shaking around in the chair to set himself free. A voice comes through the darkness facing him.

"No need for you to do such a thing." A voice echoed.

Timothy stops shaking and stares into the darkness. Looking for the location of the voice. Squinting his eyes.

"Who's there? Speak again."

The footsteps are heard once more. Only this time, Timothy can see the boots coming into the light and after several more steps, Timothy can see the one who spoke to him. A middle-aged man. Rugged in appearance, wearing cargo attire with a sleeveless shirt with scruffy facial hair and a almost shaved head. The man was the leader of the Renegades.

"Here I am."

Timothy looked. Seeing Castle in front of him. From all around Timothy and Castle enter into the light the other renegades. About a dozen of them.

"As you can see, you're not alone."

"Why am I tied to this chair?"

"Few of the watch guards caught you roaming through the Desolate, alone. They believed you to be a shell for the realm guards. You're not one of them are you?"

"I am not one of them." Timothy replied.

"Your uniform represents the Realm. Therefore, it makes you a loyal subject to the Dictator."

Timothy gazed down at his uniform. He even looked around, scanning the renegades' own attire. He knew they could tell the difference between the ones who are aligned with the Dictator and those who are the renegades. The apparel of the renegades were cargo pants and militaristic vests. Both dirty and wet from water.

"I see your reasoning, Mr.?"

"Just call me Castle. I would like to know your intent of running through the Desolate alone."

"I was told that I could find you out here. Maybe convince you to help free the others trapped in the City."

"Is that right?"

"It is." Timothy glared at the Renegades. "I can guess by your questioning that you're the leader.

"I am. Been leading the renegades ever since the fall of our freedom came to pass.

"I can see they trust you."

"Damn right they can. Most of them I been with me through the battles. Lost friends and loved ones along the way. Yet, together we stand tall."

Timothy nodded. Castle searched him, seeing if he could learn Timothy's motives.

"Tell me why you're here? Honestly."

"I escaped the confines of the City and ran into the Desolate. That's how your watch guards spotted me. I was told to find renegades by a mechroid."

Castle looked intrigued. Crossing his arms.

"What kind of mechroid?"

"An espionage mechroid. Operated with the technology within the City."

"Did it have a name?"

"Yeah."

"Tell me its name."

"That's not important. I can attest to that."

Castle stared at Timothy. His arms steady. No movement and little emotion.

"Why?"

"Try me."

Timothy nodded.

"A14-12. That was its name."

Castle looked over at the other renegades. They turned and spoke to each other before Castle focused his attention back to Timothy. Timothy could see the seriousness in Castle's eyes. Castle bent down toward Timothy, looking him in the eyes. Timothy shook with a certain fear. Castle's presence was something to fear. Even some of the renegades feared him.

"Where is this mechroid now?"

"Still in the City."

Castle grinned.

"I'm not certain to take what you've told me as fact."

"It's all true. That's the only reason I'm in this chair right now!"

"The only question is how could we enter the City when it is guarded by their snipers?"

"I…" Timothy shook. "I know a way inside the City."

"No shit." Castle scoffed.

"What I meant to say is I can take you and your group to the City. Sneak into the city and we can free the others."

Castle shook his head. Timothy couldn't tell if he accepted or rejected what he had told him. Castle stood in front of Timothy and cocked his head.

"How can we trust you?

"You can trust me. I'm not a betrayer.

"We'll know eventually. But, right now, we'll make our move into the City. And you'll be leading us in."

Timothy jerked with haste. Rattling the chair.

"Me? I don't understand?"

I'm not giving you the opportunity of bringing myself and my soldiers into death."

Timothy paused himself.

"I see your reasoning.

"That's a good start."

Castle reaches on the side of his leg and pulls out a knife. Timothy stops moving as Castle takes the knife and cuts the ropes from Timothy and the chair. Timothy sighs with relief as he stands up slowly from the chair. Castle takes the knife and places it onto Timothy's throat. Timothy gulped.

"Because if you wrong us in any way. I will personally kill you. Do you understand?"

"I understand."

Castle smiled, placing the knife back into his pocket.

"Good to know."

Castle looks to the renegades. He nods with a smirk on his face. The renegades rally up and equip themselves with their weapons, ranging from energy guns, plasma grenades, knives, and energy-coated knives." Timothy sees them gathering their weapons. Feeling uneasy as he's just walking through the area.

Outside of the base, the renegades are sitting on dirt bikes, preparing to ride off toward the Realm's City. Timothy himself gets onto a bike. Castle sees him on the bike and points at him.

"You get in the front!" Castle pointed outward.

"You and your soldiers have the firepower." Timothy replied. "Why do I have to be in the front?"

"Get your ass in the front!"

Timothy went and sat atop the bike in front of them. Castle gave the renegades the command to follow.

The renegades had reached the city. They paused for a moment and Castle turns over to Timothy. Pointing at the city. Glancing up to the skyscraper structure and moving crafts.

"Lead us in."

"Of course. Follow along quietly. Hide your bikes over near the walls. The guards rarely do searches on this side of the city."

"Hide the bikes." Castle commanded the Renegades.

The renegades leave their bikes next to the wall. The wall is made up of a mixture between bricks and titanium wiring. The wiring glowed various colors with electricity flowing through it. It appears as if it was meant to be a twisted, yet somewhat beautiful sight to outsiders. Timothy guided Castle and the renegades toward the location where he had exited the city during his escape. The surroundings were clear as Timothy opened the door and they entered into the corridor.

Castle walked behind Timothy while the other renegades watched every corner. Prepared to fire.

"I have to ask you, kid. Why are you involved in all of this?"

"It's all a mistake." Timothy answered.

"A mistake? Saving others from tyranny is no mistake."

Timothy stops and faces Castle. Castle reads his eyes. He senses something within him. Hidden behind his outward visage.

"I see. You're a deserter."

Timothy took note and continued walking.

"You turned against the Realm and for good reason."

"I turned against them because of the destruction they plan to bring."

"They've always plotted destruction. It's nothing new."

"Be that as it may. It doesn't spare me from the death I will receive."

"Death is only a solution of theirs. To trigger fear. What you've done, whether it is out of cowardice or bravery, it's for a greater cause."

Timothy listened to Castle's words closely.

"Hope I don't screw it up."

"You won't. You've shown me enough to figure that."

Walking through the corridor slowly, Timothy returned to the room A14-12 was in. Timothy enters the room with a storming haste.

The electric room is the base for the City's primary grid system. The walls glowing with a bluish hue as the energy flows through the wiring. Timothy looks around the room, but A14-12 is nowhere to be seen. Castle enters the room and looks around. Seeing the amount of tech that sat within its walls.

Castle scanned the room entirely. His eyes keen to the doorways.

"Look at this stuff."

Timothy looked over toward Castle. Shaking his head. Castle doesn't understand what Timothy's problem is or what he's trying to say.

"What is it?"

"The mechroid isn't here."

"Maybe it went to help the others find a way out."

"Maybe."

Not finding the mechroid, Timothy led them outside of the electric room.

As they step out into the corridor, on the other end are realm guards. Staring down Timothy, Castle, and the renegades. Their energy guns are searing and buzzing. Prepared for fire.

"Well, I'll be damned. We have company."

One of the realm guards raised up his plasma-range.

"Renegades! You have one request. Surrender yourselves now and come with us to be questioned and judged."

Castle stood firm. Determined about his next move as were the Renegades.

"I'm not going anywhere with you."

"We will now respond in the proper circumstance."

Castle stood his ground with the renegades. The realm guards begin firing toward the renegades. They run across the corridor. Some enter the electric room. Castle fires back at the guards with the renegades. Flying energy blasts zooming across the corridor back and forth. Timothy ran out of the corridor and into another doorway, which led down into another corridor.

Timothy ran through the second corridor and as he reaches its end, he bumps into A14-12. Standing around the robot are humans, beaten and battered, looking to escape. Timothy smiled.

"Where were you earlier?"

"I was preparing to aid these people for escape."

"How would you get them out?"

"I knew you were coming back with the renegades."

"How?" Timothy asked.

"I have my ways."

Timothy nods and leads them out of the corridor and toward the exit. He opens the door and the people barge out of the corridor.

"Get away from this place as far as you can."

The people run outside and towards the Desolate. Timothy and A14 return to the first corridor, where they can hear the echoes of firing energy blasts. Nearing the doorway, the blasts slowly cease and turn into silence. Timothy, hesitant to open the door, opens it anyway. Timothy and A14 enter the first corridor and within the corridor are dead renegades and dead guards. They look and see Castle with several other renegades exit the electric room. Castle smiles and laughs as he approaches Timothy and A14.

"Where did you go?"

"I helped A14 set some humans free." Timothy looked around. "I see that you've managed to take them out."

"As you can see, I lost some of my own. Enough as I can manage at the moment."

Timothy turned to A14 as did Castle.

"We must leave this place now. She's coming."

"Who's coming?" Timothy wondered.

Castle shakes his head looking at Timothy as they proceed to exit the corridor and return to the outside.

"You mean to tell me that you don't know who "she" is?"

Timothy stood confused.

"I don't know who A14 is talking about. Who is this "she"?"

"We must hurry."

"Who is she?" Timothy asked.

They approach the exit door and open it. Running to the outside of the City.

Running outside, they find themselves chased by drones and several realm guards. Castle sees it and isn't happy about it. His face twists with anger and haste.

"Damn!" Castle yelled.

"This isn't good."

"You don't say."

A14 starts to beep as they get on the bikes. The mechroid can sense someone approaching them near the realm guards. A14 knows of that peculiar presence.

"Here she comes."

"I'm asking, who is she?"

Castle turned to face the guards. It was there he saw her in the distance. The footsteps sounded rough against the dirt. With vigor.

"Look ahead, kid." Castle pointed.

Timothy looks and see her. A woman dressed in all grey. Her dark hair down to her shoulders. Her eyes glowing of emerald. He lips red as blood. Her countenance as wicked as one could read. She is the Dictator.

They ride off into the Desolate as realm guards approach the Dictator. Bowing before her presence.

"Should we pursue them, my Lady?"

"No need." The Dictator grinned. "Everything is in proper order."

The realm guards returned to the City while the Dictator stared, watching the bikes ride out further into the Desolate.

THE NEXT ENTRY INTO THE LITHONIA SAGA...

THE LITHONIAN WARS

AVAILABLE NOW!

ABOUT THE AUTHOR

Ty'Ron W. C. Robinson II is the author of several works of fiction. Including the *Dark Titan Universe Saga*, *The Haunted City Saga*, *EverWar Universe*, *Symbolum Venatores*, *Frightened!*, *Instincts,* and others. More information pertaining to the author and stories can be found at darktitanentertainment.com.

Gettr: @TyronRobinsonII

Twitter: @DarkTitan_
Instagram: @darktitanentertainment
Facebook: @DarkTitanEnt
Pinterest: @darktitanentertainment
YouTube: Dark Titan Entertainment
Rumble: Dark Titan Entertainment

www.ingramcontent.com/pod-product-compliance
Lightning Source LLC
LaVergne TN
LVHW041558070526
838199LV00046B/2032